P9-CNF-737

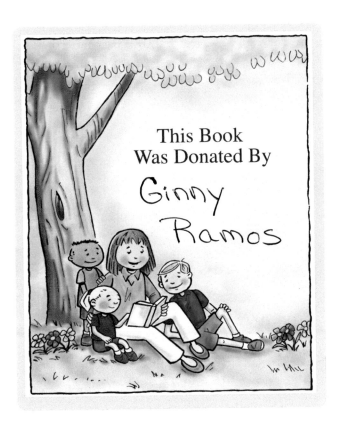

This Book
Was Donated By

Ginny
Ramos

Dax Dragonfly

Becomes...Himself

Written and Illustrated by
Julia Ramus O'Shaughnessy

For Colin, who inspired me to draw again, and for Kevin, whose support and encouragement made this project possible.

Dax Dragonfly

Becomes...Himself

Written and Illustrated by
Julia Ramus O'Shaughnessy

"Don't even think about taking another step, Skinny Boy," sneered the leader. "Why don't you take those fancy wings of yours and go flutter with the ladybugs!"

Dax tried to choke back his tears when he realized that, for the third time that week, the Bully Bugs weren't going to budge. But thinking of his worried mama and the cold dinner that would await him sent a trickle down his cheek.

"I hate being a dragonfly,"
he sniffled, turning to take the long
way home. "I wish I were an
actual dragon."

"Then I'd have super-strong

TOUGH-GUY ARMS

– and RAZOR-SHARP TALONS!"

"There would be

nothing fluttery about the

of *these* leathery wings."

And then,
Dax imagined,
he'd prance home,
feeling powerful
and *oh-so-proud*--

--though getting through
the door might be
a bit of a squeeze.

While no one could make him late for dinner, that blazing breath would seriously stamp out his meal's appeal.

Nights would be
uncomfortably long.

Worst of all,

even if he was very, very careful,

his favorite lovey would never

look at him in the same way.

"Hmmm..."

Dax paused as he considered the hardships of life as an actual dragon.

"On second thought..."

He stood up taller
and puffed out his chest.

"Actually,
I *like* being Dax Dragonfly –
just the way I am."

66289677R00017

Made in the USA
Lexington, KY
10 August 2017